P9-DGW-454

Written by Helen L. Wilbur and Illustrated by John Manders

For Blue Mama and Pop, their children and grandchildren
—Helen

For Gabby
—John

Author's Acknowledgments
Special thanks to the men, women, and horses of mounted units everywhere.

Sleeping Bear Press™
315 E. Eisenhower Parkway, Suite 200
Ann Arbor, MI 48108
www.sleepingbearpress.com

Printed and bound in the United States.

10 9 8 7 6 5 4 3 2 1

Library of Congress Cataloging-in-Publication Data

Wilbur, Helen L., 1948-
Finnegan and Fox : the ten-foot cop / written by Helen L. Wilbur ; illustrated by John Manders.
p. cm.
Summary: When a child goes missing in New York City's Times Square, Finnegan the police horse leads his partner, Fox, to the rescue.
ISBN 978-1-58536-784-9
1. Police horses–Juvenile fiction. [1. Police horses–Fiction. 2. Horses–Fiction. 3. Missing children–Fiction. 4. Policemen–Fiction. 5. New York (N.Y.)–Fiction.] I. Manders, John, ill. II. Title.
PZ10.3.W6513Fin 2013
[Fic]–dc23 2012033576

My name is Finnegan. I am ten years old, weigh 1,256 pounds, and wear steel shoes. I am a proud member of the New York City Police Department. Times Square is my beat.

Meet my partner, Tyrone Jefferson Fox—we call him T. J. but it's Officer Fox to you. T. J. grew up right here in New York City and plays a mean game of basketball. Together we make a ten-foot-tall policeman. The NYPD Mounted Unit takes only the best—horses or officers.

You've got to have a calm temperament and a cool head to make the grade and patrol the Big Apple. We horses are naturally nervous and likely to run when frightened.

Months of training at the NYPD remount school get us ready to face any situation with confidence and control, whether it's handling a rowdy crowd at a ball game or marching in formation down Fifth Avenue in a parade. With our human partners we can see and be seen in the crowded streets.

Not everyone feels comfortable around a police officer. People can be annoying. But who doesn't like a horse?

After graduation we get assigned to our partners. Officers who have just finished training, along with those whose mounts have retired, get a chance to look us over. I want a partner who's smart and steady so I'm putting my best hoof forward.

One officer circles me slowly, really taking his time. He's a tall guy, his uniform is crisp and his badge shines. He checks me out from forelock to tail, running a cool, firm hand along my flank, asking the trainer all about me.

"His name is Finnegan. He's steady and strong but he can be ornery. He has a mind of his own," the trainer says.

"Well, I guess that makes us a match. Let's go, Finnegan," T. J. says as he swings onto my saddle. We've been a team ever since.

Our day starts in the new stables on Pier 76 near the Hudson River. The hostlers take care of us, get us fed, brushed, and polished up so we are as neat and trim as our human partners. T. J. checks my hooves, gives my mane and tail a final brushing (he likes us to look extra handsome) and saddles me up. T. J. attends roll call, gets our instructions for the day, then off we go.

Hassan is on the corner with his fruit and vegetable cart and a pile of tasty-looking apples. He waves to T. J. and me. But no treats on patrol.

Next we pass Officer Serafina Ruiz directing traffic out of the Lincoln Tunnel. She blows her whistle hard and always gives T. J. a big smile.

Mrs. Waxman walks her dog, Murray. She flutters her fingers as we go by. "Good morning, Officer Fox and you, too, Finnegan." Murray growls.

The big blue and yellow umbrella means that T. J. will stop for his morning coffee from Tony. "Yo, Finnegan," Tony says and strokes my head as T. J. takes a sip.

It's 8 a.m. Times Square is filled with people. A million and a half people go through Times Square every day so I guess they have to start early. New Yorkers rush by on their way to work but tourists stop and look and take pictures. The buildings aren't the only popular sight. Every few blocks, someone stops to say hello.

"What's your horse's name?"

"Can I pet him?"

"Can my dad take our picture?"

What can I say? We are celebrities.

For many city kids we are the first horses they get to see up close. T. J. lets them pet my neck and head. Their smiles shine as they repeat my name, "Finnegan, hey there, Finnegan, nice horse." Sometimes I give them a little nicker and shake my head.

Today a group of kids on a school visit surrounds us and asks T. J. all sorts of questions about me.

"What breed is he?"

"What feed do you give him?"

"What kind of saddle is that?"

These guys clearly know their horses.

And no wonder. When T. J. asks, "Where are you guys from?" the answer is a loud:

"CHEYENNE, WYOMING!"

One of the mothers leans in with a little girl in her arms. "Hey, Maggie, look, a horse right in the middle of New York City."

Maggie reaches out for my mane, presses her face against my head, and murmurs my name. It doesn't get sweeter than that. "She just loves horses," her mother says.

An ambulance whines in the distance and flashing lights come into view.
We fan out with Officer McNally and her mount Eddie to clear the way.

T. J. spots a car with an outdated inspection sticker and writes a ticket.

A van marked “Cakes in Motion” stops next to us. The driver leans out the window.

“Officer, can you direct us to the Plaza Hotel? We have a wedding cake to deliver and we don’t want to be late.” T. J. tells him the best route so the cake will arrive on time. “Good luck!” he calls after them.

We ride by to see construction workers
digging deep into the earth to build a new office
tower. A scream gets everyone's attention. T. J. and I turn and a
young woman grabs T. J.'s boot.

"Something ran over my foot!" she cries.

Sure enough a little mouse scuttles across the street and disappears
between the buildings.

"You are okay, Miss. It won't hurt you." She starts to calm down.

“By the way,” T. J. asks, “where are you from?”

“New Jersey,” she says.

“Well, be careful, we don’t like out-of-towners scaring our mice.” Everyone laughs, especially the young woman, then they all go on their way.

There's a lot to do on patrol and the day passes quickly. After lunch T. J.'s radio crackles an alert. A child is lost and we've been called in for the search.

An officer passes out flyers with a photo. It's little Maggie from Wyoming.

"We believe she just slipped away when her mother's back was turned so she can't be far. With all the people in the streets, someone must have noticed a little girl all by herself. Fox, double-check this area," he points to the map and off we go.

LOST
LOST
LOST
LOST
NYPD

The first minutes of a search are precious ones. The group from Wyoming has already been through this block calling Maggie's name but T. J. follows procedure and starts to investigate.

T. J. dismounts to talk to a storekeeper. "Stand, Finnegan," he says as he fastens my reins.

I'm trained to stay and not fiddle with my reins. But there's something down the alley I want to look at. I pull hard and walk down the alleyway toward a pile of cardboard boxes.

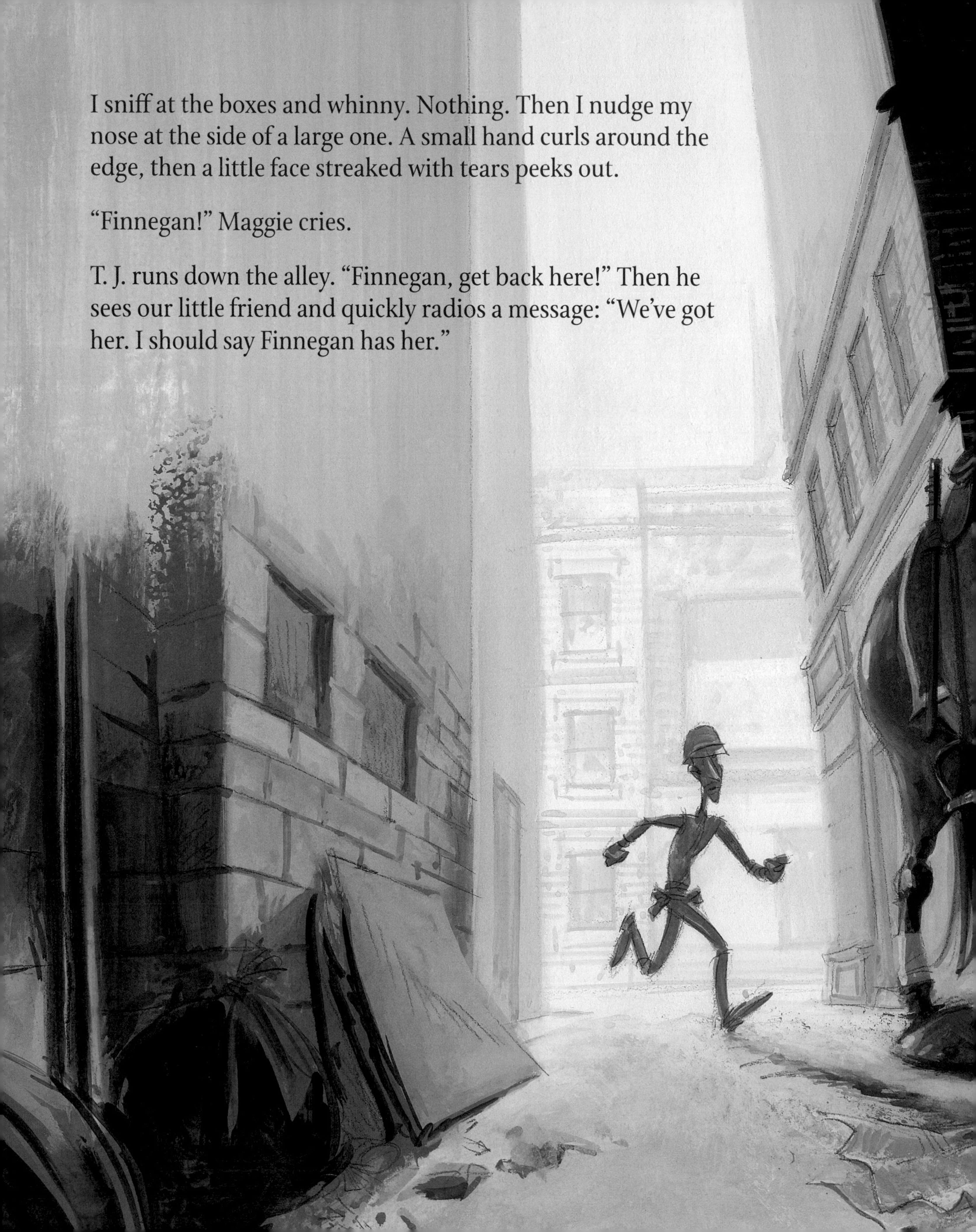

I sniff at the boxes and whinny. Nothing. Then I nudge my nose at the side of a large one. A small hand curls around the edge, then a little face streaked with tears peeks out.

"Finnegan!" Maggie cries.

T. J. runs down the alley. "Finnegan, get back here!" Then he sees our little friend and quickly radios a message: "We've got her. I should say Finnegan has her."

In a few minutes the alley is filled with people and with cameras. Maggie's parents hug her and me.

"Oh, Finnegan," her mother cries. "All the strangers calling Maggie's name scared her so she hid in the box. But she wasn't afraid of you. Finnegan, you are our hero!"

now.
04 43

Well, they make a big fuss out of me. T. J., too. By the time we ride back through Times Square our photo has already been sent to the huge digital news sign looming over the square. People cheer us as we go by. But it's all part of our job.

We head home for a shower, a good brushing, a dinner of our special feed, and maybe a nice treat.

Tony's closing up his cart for the day but raises his fist for a bump and shouts, "Way to go, Finnegan!"

Mrs. Waxman calls, "We are so proud of you!" She holds up Murray, who greets us with a yip.

"Hey, Finnegan and Fox, you guys are heroes!" Officer Ruiz beams as we go by. Her eyes are sparkling … and so are T. J.'s.

As we turn the corner to the stable, T. J. says,
"Finnegan, look, someone has a reward for you."

I can see that Hassan is holding out a juicy red apple.

More Information about Mounted Police

Mounted Police

In police forces all over the world, mounted units play an important role in crime prevention, ceremonies, and public relations. Such diverse places as Brazil, Barbados, India, Lesotho, Bulgaria, France, Israel, Malta, and New Zealand, to name a few, use the majestic presence and gentle bearing of the horse and rider to control as well as to charm the public.

Mounted patrols serve as color guards in parades and ceremonies. Their size and stature make them effective in seeing over crowds as well as managing large groups of people. A horse and rider make a "ten-foot cop." Besides their utility in law enforcement, police horses create tremendous goodwill in public relations. Who doesn't like a horse?

Search and Rescue

Mounted units perform an important part in patrolling remote areas inaccessible by vehicle. Used in search and rescue, horses can move fast in isolated areas. Horses also have a well-developed sense of smell which can assist in finding lost persons. Border patrols use mounted units to control smuggling. In the desert countries like Jordan and Egypt, mounted police ride camels.

United States and Canada

Founded in 1871, the Mounted Unit of the New York City Police Department is the oldest and largest in North America. The legendary Royal Canadian Mounted Police were formed only two years later in 1873.

Mounted patrols operate in remote areas, large and small cities, on university campuses, and serve the U. S. Park Police, as well as the U. S. Border Patrol. In some communities volunteers organize mounted units and posses to support local sheriff's departments. These service organizations assist with public gatherings and emergency situations and act as ambassadors of goodwill for law enforcement.

Training

Horses are intelligent, bold, and strong, with excellent memories and an ability to adapt and learn new things. The natural instinct of a horse is to run from a threat. Loud noises and unfamiliar things can spook a horse to jump, run, or buck.

A trained horse and rider make a professional team. Both horse and human recruits undergo intensive training before they join the mounted unit. Rigorous training teaches horse and rider to have trust and confidence in one another. The team gets used to working in large, often unruly, crowds. They learn to ignore sudden noises, sirens, whistles, smoke, firecrackers, shouts, flags, water, and to proceed with control and confidence in unpredictable conditions.

Qualifications for a Mounted Police Officer

First, you need to have experience on the police force. In most forces you need to finish training and serve on the force as an officer for at least two years before applying for a specialist department such as the mounted police. The good news is that you need not have experience with horses to qualify. General fitness and a good record are paramount. The department will teach you how to ride and handle a horse.

Recruit training isn't all glamour. It is hard work involving cleaning stables and tack as well as spending many hours a day in the saddle.

Retirement

When horses retire from active duty, nonprofit agencies, as well as the police departments, find them new homes. Several police agencies run ranches and farms specifically to care for retired horses.